Suddenly, Doc's brother Donny bursts into her room, pushing his toy fire engine with Lambie on board.

Quick as a flash, Doc's toys go stuffed!

"Will you play firefighters with me?" Donny asks.

"Maybe later, okay?" says Doc.

Doc picks up Lambie and Stuffy as Donny leaves.

Doc hurries out to the back garden.
"I'm going outside to play, Mum!" she calls.
"Okay, sweetie," Doc's mum says. "Just take care.
It's a very hot day!"
"I will," Doc answers.

Doc McStuffins opens the door to her clinic
and turns round the welcome sign.
"The Doc is in!" she says.

"Hi, Hallie!" says Doc. "Do we have any toys that need fixing?"
"No patients yet," answers Hallie. "My, my – it sure is hot today."
"It's even too hot to cuddle," says Lambie.

Just then, Squeakers bounces through the door.
"Squeak, squeak, squeeeeaaak!"
"What's he saying?" Stuffy asks.
"I don't know. I don't speak squeak," says Hallie.
Doc has an idea. "Squeakers, can you *show* us what's wrong?"

Squeakers leads Doc and the others into the back garden.
"What's wrong with you, Engine Nine?" says Donny.
He pumps Lenny's siren and points the hose at a pretend fire,
but nothing comes out!
"Oh no," says Donny. "You're broken!"

Donny puts Lenny on a pile of broken toys.

"Sorry, Lenny," he says sadly. "You were an awesome toy.
I'm going to miss you."

"Awww, Donny looks so sad," says Doc.

"I know how you can cheer up Donny," says Lambie.

"Fix Lenny!" Stuffy says.

When Donny has left, Doc and the toys run to Lenny.

"What's wrong, Lenny?" asks Stuffy.

"I keep running out of water," Lenny says. "A fire engine that can't put out a fire isn't much good."

"Let's get you to the clinic, Lenny," Doc says. "It's time for a check-up!"

Lenny is a little nervous. "What is a check-up?" he asks.
"It's when a doctor takes a look at you to make sure you're
healthy," says Lambie.
Doc listens to Lenny's heartbeat.

"That sounds perfect," she says. "Lenny, has anything been bothering you lately?"

"Well, I've been feeling quite tired and my head hurts sometimes," Lenny admits. "Mostly on really hot days."

Just then, there's a knock at the door!
"Doc, I have something for you!" calls Doc's mum.
"Hurry," Doc says to her toys. "Go stuffed!"

"Hi, Mum," says Doc. "What's up?"

"I brought you some water, sweetie," says Doc's mum. "I don't want you to get dehydrated."

"What's dehydrated?" Doc asks.

"If you don't drink enough water, especially on a hot day, you can feel sick."

"Dehydrated," repeats Doc. "That's it! Thanks, Mum."

"Lenny, you have Driedout-a-tosis!" announces Doc.

"Oh, my! That sounds like it should go straight into the Big Book of Boo-Boos!" says Hallie.

"What does Driedout-a-tosis mean, Doc?" asks Lenny.

"It's like being dehydrated – when you aren't drinking enough water," Doc explains. "Drinking water is important, especially when it's hot!"

Doc puts a glass of water in front of Lenny.

"Drink it all up," she says.

"Ah," says Lenny. "I feel better already!"

Hallie looks into Lenny's fire hose. "Is this thing working now?" she asks. "Yep, it sure as stuffin' is!" laughs Hallie.

Donny is surprised to see Doc with his fire engine.
"Engine Nine! What are you doing here?"
Lenny shoots a stream of water out of his hose.
"Awesome!" Donny shouts. "You're working again!
I missed you."

"Help! Help!" shouts Doc. "We have to rescue Stuffy from the burning building!"

"Don't worry, Stuffy," yells Donny. "Engine Nine will save you!"

Donny points Lenny's hose at the pretend fire and water gushes out! "Whoa! Great job, Engine Nine!" Donny says.

"Thanks for playing with me, Doc," Donny says.
"You're the best sister ever."
"I love hanging out with you, Donny," says Doc.
"And our toys do, too!"